✔ KU-167-188

Scholastic Publications Ltd.,
10 Earlham Street, London WC2H 9RX, UK

Scholastic Inc.,
730 Broadway, New York, NY 10003, USA

Scholastic Tab Publications Ltd.,
123 Newkirk Road, Richmond Hill,
Ontario L4C 3G5, Canada

Ashton Scholastic Pty. Ltd.,
P O Box 579, Gosford, New South Wales,
Australia

Ashton Scholastic Ltd.,
165 Marua Road, Panmure, Auckland 6,
New Zealand

First published by Scholastic Publications Limited, 1989
Text copyright © Scholastic Publications Limited, 1989
Illustrations copyright © Scholastic Publications Limited, 1989

ISBN 0 590 85865 3

Made and printed in Hong Kong
Typeset in Times Roman by AKM Associates (UK) Ltd,
Ajmal House, Hayes Road, Southall, London

A Cat called Curiosity and Other Tales

Stories by **Geoffrey Alan**

Artist **Valeria Petrone**

Hippo Books
Scholastic Publications Ltd
London

Smudge

The cat stopped, one paw poised in mid-air. Ears and whiskers twitching, it listened and sniffed. Then, silently, it trotted on its way, behind the stables.

Suddenly, a dog's face appeared round the corner. Next moment, its fur bristling, the cat turned and darted away. Barking loudly, the dog gave chase.

Kate and her parents heard the commotion. So did Kate's pony, Pickles, and he shied nervously.

"Whoaa! Steady, boy!" called Kate, clinging to his halter. "Mum, what's got into Sam? He's frightening Pickles."

"He never usually barks near the horses," replied Mum, helping Sally hold Pickles. "He must have spotted something."

Seeking cover, the cat sped through the open stable-door. But as Sam came skidding and sliding after it, stern words from Mum made him check.

"Get Pickles into the stable," said Kate's Dad. "He'll take a while to settle down."

As soon as the pony was safely inside, Kate bolted the door. There came a resounding crash as hooves and wood connected. Then a silence so sudden, that Kate and her parents looked at each other in surprise.

Within the shadows of the stable, the cat crouched low. Then the pony spotted it. The cat edged forward.

Pickles lowered his head with interest. The cat touched the pony's muzzle with the tip of its nose. It knew the pony was uneasy. Yet, as if seeking to make friends, the cat moved to one of the pony's forelegs and rubbed gently against it.

When Kate's Dad opened the stable-door, he could hardly believe his eyes.

"Look at this," he called.

The pony, now unusually quiet and relaxed, watched as the cat jumped up on some bales beside it. Then, purring loudly, the cat stepped carefully on to the pony's back. The pony whinnied softly and turned its head. But it seemed quite happy.

The cat, not the least bit nervous, curled up and closed its eyes.

"Incredible," whispered Kate's Dad. "See how calm Pickles is."

"I think that cat's a stray," said Mum. "I'm sure I've seen it in the woods."

"Not any more," said Kate. "Pickles seems to like him. So do I!"

For a moment, the cat lazily opened one eye then stretched out a paw and slept. It knew it had a home at last.

Later, Kate fetched it milk and food. The cat left Pickles long enough to eat hungrily.

Kate stroked its grey-white fur. She noticed the black patch on its head. "Like someone's spilled ink on you," she smiled. "Smudge! That's it. I shall call you Smudge!"

Over lunch, Kate and her parents could hardly stop talking about Smudge's effect on the pony.

"I'm sure Pickles just needed some company," said Kate.

"It seems that cat wants to stay, and Pickles obviously likes the idea. So it's fine by me," Dad replied.

Mum smiled, "Pickles is a strong, promising jumper. Anything that keeps him happy, especially for Saturday's gymkhana event, must be good!"

"We'll make a great team – with Smudge, too!" laughed Kate. "I'm sure he'd want Pickles to win!"

On the morning of the show, Smudge sensed the excitement. Pickles' behaviour was perfect until Dad led him towards the horse-box, hooked up to their car.

The pony warily pulled up his head, his eyes wide. Then Smudge trotted quietly into the horse-box, and Pickles followed.

Kate picked up Smudge.

"You can't come with us," she said. "But Pickles will be back soon."

Smudge watched as the trailer pulled away. Then he began to run after it.

Less than a mile away, the horse show was already beginning. Though a little uneasy at the noise and bustle, Pickles stood still while Kate saddled him up.

What happened next was just bad luck. Some bunting suddenly fell and flapped across Pickles' face. The pony reared up, startled, and Kate's Dad only just managed to stop him bolting.

15

"That's blown it!" he groaned. Pickles will never settle down in time to perform his best. Pity we didn't bring Smudge!"

Just then Smudge darted across the car park towards them. Pickles spotted him instantly.

Smudge mewed and rubbed against Pickles' legs. Kate and her parents stared amazed. Then Kate scooped up Smudge and put him in their car.

Crouched by the windscreen, Smudge watched Pickles as he calmly trotted off, with Kate, to join the other competitors.

Back home that evening, Kate proudly fingered the rosette Pickles had won.

"We've Smudge to thank, too. I still can't believe he came after us."

Smudge trotted across the room, mewed, and headed for the kitchen door.

"I can guess where he wants to go now," smiled Kate. Sure enough, Smudge hurried to the stables. As Kate and her parents followed, Smudge sprang up on the bales and then on to Pickles' back.

"He's an amazing cat," said Dad, grinning.

"Pickles thinks so, too!"

As for Smudge, he gave a little sigh then curled up and fell fast asleep.

A Cat Called Curiosity

"Where's Curiosity?" asked Jeff. "Trust him to disappear!"

"If he plays up now, Mum and Dad might change their minds about taking him with us to the caravan," replied Jan, anxiously.

"Everything packed, you two?" called Mum, carrying cases out to the car.

Suddenly, Jan remembered! "My bag!" she said, racing upstairs. Jeff followed as Jan went straight to the big hold-all she had left on her bed. The sides of the open bag seemed to ripple. Then a small, furry face with twinkly eyes popped up from inside the bag.

"Curiosity!" frowned Jan. "I guessed you couldn't resist looking in there."

"Phew! It was nearly the cattery for you," scolded Jeff, playfully. "Sticking your nose into things as usual, I see!"

Curiosity purred loudly as Jan picked him up. "Come on," she said. "We just couldn't leave you behind."

The caravan was at the far end of a large site.

"Couldn't be better!" said Mum, when they arrived. "I think we'll really enjoy it."

"So will Curiosity," said Jan.

Curiosity sat cleaning himself. Then he noticed the caravan. He trotted eagerly inside to investigate.

While exploring, Curiosity knocked over all the household items Mum had stored under the sink.

Then he dived for Dad's wardrobe, where cat and clothes became hopelessly entangled and Dad threatened to take Curiosity to the cattery, after all.

Over the next day or two, Curiosity was just as nosey outdoors.

On the first afternoon Curiosity strolled over to investigate a paint-pot, left with the lid open, by the doorstep of the nearest van. Not content with getting paint on his paws, he soon sent the can rolling over, with its contents spilling everywhere.

Then Curiosity spotted a sprinkler hose. He tapped the hose playfully with his paw. The result was a wildly writhing hose spraying water on to its startled owner.

Curiosity raced away, quite dry – but not before he had been seen!

"Let's play ball," Jeff said to Jan, afterwards.

"Don't play too near the van," Mum called. "Go over there."

She pointed to an overgrown patch of grass, beside some trees. Jan and Jeff had not gone far when Curiosity came bounding past them.

"He probably thinks there's a rabbit hole or two to explore," said Jeff.

"He'd hate to miss out on anything," said Jan.

Just ahead, Curiosity suddenly froze. His fur stood on end, then he leapt straight into the air, his legs like stiff springs.

"What. . .?" began Jeff.

"Very curious! Come on!" cried Jan.

No sooner had he landed, than Curiosity jumped again, twisting in mid-air.

Then Jeff and Jan saw something else whiplash from the grass. Curiosity moved like lightning, narrowly avoiding it.

"A snake!" shouted Jan.

Jan's Dad heard her cry and came running. Curiosity darted away from the snake, puzzled and shocked. He fled into the caravan and refused to come out.

Meanwhile, the large snake slithered off to find a quieter place, among the distant trees.

"Definitely an adder," said their Dad, watching. "I recognise the markings. It's poisonous!"

"Curiosity was lucky!" said Jeff.

"So were you two," added their Dad. "You might not have moved so fast. An adder bite can be nasty. It would mean an urgent trip to hospital."

"Poor Curiosity! He must have been scared stiff!" said Jan.

She hurried into the van to tempt him with a saucer of creamy milk.

When Mum heard the full story, she shivered. She had always been nervous of snakes. So had several of the other holidaymakers.

Jeff went with his Dad to warn them, even though the adder had probably gone for good.

For the rest of the week, Curiosity was very popular. But, he didn't seem curious about anything."

"Is he all right, Dad?" asked Jan.

"Of course," he grinned. "But we may have to give him another name."

Jeff nodded. "You're right. He's just not nosey any more."

"Give him time," smiled Mum. "Look." She held a tin closer to Curiosity. He sniffed it.

"See? You want to know what's inside, don't you?" said Mum. "You'll soon be back to normal."

Jeff, Jan and Dad all laughed.

"Don't encourage him!"

Smoky

Clare had only been at the cottage for a few days when she first saw the cat. At least, she thought she saw it. One minute it was there, the next it was gone! Puzzled, Clare was just wondering whether she had imagined the grey, almost misty outline of the cat, when she spotted it again farther down the garden.

It seemed to want to play.

"I shall call you Smoky," smiled Clare, stepping slowly towards the little creature, careful not to frighten it.

"Clare!" called her Mum. Clare spun round to answer, and in that instant the cat vanished again.

"You scared Smoky away Mum," she complained.

"Who's Smoky?" smiled Clare's Mum, walking down the garden with an elderly gentleman at her side.

"It's a cat. I think it must be a stray!"

"Where is he?" asked her Mum.

"He was here – a moment ago! He keeps appearing in different parts of the garden, especially under the yew tree. It's his favourite spot!"

"Perhaps he'll come back later," said Clare's Mum. "This is Joe. He's come to help me with the garden. He used to work for Mrs Bealton, the lady who lived here before us."

"You don't know anyone who's lost a cat, do you, Joe?" asked Clare. "A big, grey one with deep, smoky eyes. He's beautiful – and mysterious. He keeps popping up around the place."

"Can't say I do," said Joe, rubbing a crooked finger on his chin. "Mrs Bealton had a cat just like that though. He loved the garden. He always used to lie under the yew tree."

Clare felt a tingle run down her spine.

"Fact is, the cat died same day as Mrs Bealton passed away."

"Er, well, Clare, it's time for your tea. Thank you for calling, Joe. We'll see you in the morning then."

While Clare made her way to the kitchen, her mind was full of Joe's story.

"Mum, you don't suppose Smoky – I mean the cat I keep seeing – is Mrs Bealton's?"

"How can it be, dear?" asked her Mum. "You heard what Joe said. . ."

"That's what I meant, Mum – a ghost cat!"

"Nonsense!" Mum shook her head. Any cat would like to sit under the yew tree. It's the best shady spot in the whole garden."

Next morning, Clare was up early exploring the garden again.

"Smoky! Smoky!" she called. "Where are you? Oh, all right! If you don't want to come and play. . ."

Smoky did not appear. As Clare looked for him, she spotted a corner of the garden that she had not seen before. It was hidden from view by overgrown brambles. In it, she saw a tree, heavily-laden with plums.

"M'm! Mum'll be pleased," thought Clare. "Just wait till I tell her."

Just then, Joe arrived.

"Mum! Mum! I've found some plums. Come and see this tree!" shouted Clare, waving from down the garden. She turned and ran out of sight.

Suddenly, a look of alarm flashed across Joe's eyes.

"No, stop! Come back, missy! Wait!"

Clare could not hear him clearly. Besides, she wanted to try a plum.

"I'll have to climb the tree," she thought. "If I can just reach that first branch. . ."

Clare spotted what looked like an old wooden gate lying in the long grass.

"I could lean it against the tree-trunk," she said, "and then pull myself up into the tree."

But as Clare began to move a shadow above her made her look up.

"Smoky!" she smiled. The cat had climbed to the very end of a long branch in the plum tree, and as Clare gasped, Smoky leapt.

He sprang right past Clare's face. Clare was forced to take a step or two backwards. The cat landed, ran through her legs and on a few yards. Then it stopped, glancing back to see if Clare would follow.

"So you *do* want to play," said Clare, forgetting about the plum tree.

Next moment, Joe arrived, followed by Clare's Mum.

"Don't move!" shouted Joe. "The old well. Some years ago, I boarded it over for Mrs Bealton."

Carefully, Joe edged towards what Clare had thought was the old gate.

"That's the lid I made!" said Joe. He kicked the edge of it with his boot. Rotted timber split and the lid fell . . . down . . . down . . . Far below, in the deep shaft, they heard wooden splinters hitting water.

"Clare! You might have had a terrible accident. No one ever told us about the well," her Mum cried.

"I would have stepped right over it . . . and fallen, if Smoky hadn't stopped me!" said Clare, shaken.

"You mean that cat?" asked her Mum.

Joe scratched his chin. "Mrs Bealton's cat knew that well. He'd watch his mistress pull up a bucket. She'd use it to water the flowers down here.

"Mum, then that cat . . . it was a ghost!" gasped Clare.

Certainly, Smoky had vanished again.

Next morning, when Joe turned up for work, he saw Clare stroking a grey cat.

"Ghost, indeed!" laughed Clare's Mum. "It's your stray cat. I told you, didn't I? He's welcome to stay as long as he likes!"

"I'm still not sure," began Clare. "I suppose you're right, Mum. He does look the same."

Even as they watched, the stray settled under the yew tree and began to clean ifself.

"I wonder. . .?" Joe muttered quietly to himself.